Welcome to Horse-riding Club

T0337176

Written by Claire Llewellyn

Illustrated by Rupert Van Wyk

Collins

Who and what is in this story?

Listen and say

🎧 One day, Jo sees a new girl at horse-riding club.

Jo shows Mary her horse. She says,
"I ride Coco."

Jo says, "You ride Chip."
Mary says, "OK, thanks."

Jo says, "Let's clean our horses."

Jo says, "This is how you brush a horse."

OK, I can do that.

Jo says, "This is how you clean a horse's feet."

Yes, OK.

11

Then Jo and Mary get saddles.

Jo says, "This is how you put the saddle on."

"Then you put on your riding hat."

Yes, I know.

Jo says, "This is how you get on a horse. Why don't you try?"

Mary gets on her horse.

Jo and Mary are riding their horses.

Jo says, "No, Mary, walk behind! You can learn from me."

Jo is showing Mary how to jump.

Look at me, Mary!

Mary doesn't see.

Let's go, Chip!

Mary is jumping with Chip.
She knows how to ride a horse.
She's a good rider.

And she knows how to jump, too!

Picture dictionary

Listen and repeat

brush

clean

horse

horse-riding

jump

rider

riding hat

saddle

1 Look and order the story

2 Listen and say

Download a reading guide for parents and teachers at
www.collins.co.uk/839776

Collins

Published by Collins
An imprint of HarperCollins*Publishers*
Westerhill Road
Bishopbriggs
Glasgow
G64 2QT

HarperCollins*Publishers*
1st Floor, Watermarque Building
Ringsend Road
Dublin 4
Ireland

William Collins' dream of knowledge for all began with the publication of his first book in 1819.

A self-educated mill worker, he not only enriched millions of lives, but also founded a flourishing publishing house. Today, staying true to this spirit, Collins books are packed with inspiration, innovation and practical expertise. They place you at the centre of a world of possibility and give you exactly what you need to explore it.

© HarperCollins*Publishers* Limited 2020

10 9 8 7 6 5 4 3 2

ISBN 978-0-00-839776-0

Collins® and COBUILD® are registered trademarks of HarperCollins*Publishers* Limited

www.collins.co.uk/elt

All rights reserved. No part of this publication may be reproduced, stored in a retrieval system, or transmitted in any form by any means, electronic, mechanical, photocopying, recording or otherwise, without the prior written permission of the Publisher or a licence permitting restricted copying in the United Kingdom issued by the Copyright Licensing Agency Ltd, 5th Floor, Shackleton House, 4 Battle Bridge Lane, London SE1 2HX.

British Library Cataloguing in Publication Data

A catalogue record for this publication is available from the British Library.

All rights reserved. No part of this book may be reproduced, stored in a retrieval system, or transmitted in any form or by any means, electronic, mechanical, photocopying, recording or otherwise, without the prior permission in writing of the Publisher. This book is sold subject to the conditions that it shall not, by way of trade or otherwise, be lent, re-sold, hired out or otherwise circulated without the Publisher's prior consent in any form of binding or cover other than that in which it is published and without a similar condition including this condition being imposed on the subsequent purchaser.

Author: Claire Llewellyn
Illustrator: Rupert Van Wyk (Beehive)
Series editor: Rebecca Adlard
Commissioning editor: Fiona Undrill
Publishing manager: Lisa Todd
Product managers: Jennifer Hall and Caroline Green
In-house editor: Alma Puts Keren
Project manager: Emily Hooton
Editor: Barbara MacKay
Proofreaders: Natalie Murray and Michael Lamb
Cover designer: Kevin Robbins
Typesetter: 2Hoots Publishing Services Ltd
Audio produced by id audio, London
Reading guide author: Emma Wilkinson
Production controller: Rachel Weaver
Printed and bound by: GPS Group, Slovenia

MIX
Paper from
responsible sources
FSC™ C007454

This book is produced from independently certified FSC™ paper to ensure responsible forest management.

For more information visit: **www.harpercollins.co.uk/green**

Download the audio for this book and a reading guide for parents and teachers at www.collins.co.uk/839776